SURVIVING
TERROR

TRUE TEEN STORIES FROM AROUND THE WORLD

True Teen Stories from

**Surviving
Civil War**

Kristin Thiel

New York

Published in 2019 by Cavendish Square Publishing, LLC
243 5th Avenue, Suite 136, New York, NY 10016

First Edition

Website: cavendishsq.com

Library of Congress Cataloging-in-Publication Data

Names: Thiel, Kristin, 1977- author.
Title: True teen stories from Syria : surviving civil war / Kristin Thiel.
Other titles: Surviving civil war
Description: First edition. | New York, NY : Cavendish Square Publishing, LLC, 2019. | Series: Surviving terror: true teen stories from around the world
Identifiers: LCCN 2017058839 (print) | LCCN 2018004520 (ebook) | ISBN 9781502635426 (e-Book) | ISBN 9781502635419 (library bound) | ISBN 9781502635433 (pbk.)
Subjects: LCSH: Syria--History--Civil War, 2011---Juvenile literature. | Syria--History--Civil War, 2011---Youth--Juvenile literature. | Teenage soldiers--Syria--History--21st century--Juvenile literature. | Teenagers--Syria--History--21st century--Juvenile literature. | Terrorism--Syria--History--21st century--Juvenile literature.
Classification: LCC DS98.6 (ebook) | LCC DS98.6 .T47 2019 (print) | DDC 956.9104/23092535--dc23
LC record available at https://lccn.loc.gov/2017058839

Editorial Director: David McNamara
Editor: Caitlyn Miller
Copy Editor: Rebecca Rohan
Associate Art Director: Amy Greenan
Designer: Alan Sliwinski
Production Assistant: Karol Szymczuk
Photo Research: J8 Media

Printed in the United States of America

CONTENTS

A girl walks through the town of Arbin, near Syria's capital of Damascus, in 2016.

CHAPTER ONE

SYRIA AND CIVIL WAR

Syria's rich history traces back to ancient times. It has been a settled area for thousands of years, but it's only been considered a nation-state, or country, since the early 1900s. (For simplicity, it will be referred to as Syria in this book, even during discussion of its early years.) It sits in a region of the world known for its historical significance, cultural richness, and natural resources, as well as its political strife. Today, the nation of Syria faces devastating challenges due to a civil war that began in 2011. For teens growing up there, day-to-day life poses both unique challenges and moments of hope and normalcy.

People enjoy the historic downtown of Aleppo in 2010, before the war.

Teenagers in War

The one situation in Syria that affects everyone, including young people, is the bloody civil war that's been raging for nearly a decade. What started as protests by its citizens against Syria's oppressive regime has become a broad and gruesome conflict, with multiple factions fighting both the government and each other, sometimes with the involvement of other countries' governments and groups. According to Mercy Corps, a humanitarian aid agency, by late 2017, at least 470,000 people have been killed since the war started. The United Nations estimated that 11 million Syrians have fled their homes—that is half of the country's prewar population. Of those, 4.8 million are now refugees outside of Syria.

Teens have become wrapped up in every aspect of this war. In fact, one daring late-night act by a group of teenagers helped to ignite what would become the Syrian Civil War. As the fighting continues, young people have been forced to become soldiers or refugees.

Pastor Samuel, with the organization Open Doors USA, is a church leader in Aleppo, one of Syria's major cities that has been devastated by the war. About four years into the fighting, he met with several teenagers. He wanted to learn what their daily lives were like.

They reported being scared of bombs, rockets, being injured, and their families dying. Still, they also had hopes for their futures. They imagined attending college and landing good jobs. The question "What does a regular day look like for you?" elicited a surprising answer: "Boring. Things make no sense at all. Every day is the same boring day. There is nothing to do for us and no place to go except going to school—if the situation allows us. There is nothing exciting, nothing new." Life for Syrians is not actually boring, but the realities of war have become so real to them that they're now commonplace. Syrians have become skillful at leading "regular" lives among the strangeness of war. In some ways, that is one of the most terrifying stories of teenagers in Syria.

There is a generation of people growing up not knowing anything of peace, safety, or prosperity.

This would be a tragedy anywhere. In a place like Syria, the tragedy is uniquely layered. The country is in a powerhouse position in the world. It is one of the oldest civilizations. Its location at the meeting point of Europe, Asia, and Africa has made it a part of important trading routes since the beginning of humanity. The Syrian Civil War is destroying an important part of our world—and its irreplaceable people. Syria has also never been an easy place

Syria borders Iraq, Jordan, Israel, Lebanon, and Turkey.

to live. Many different groups have engaged in war there and occupied the area. The land and weather often create inhospitable—difficult, even dangerous—living conditions. Syria is not a stranger to tragedy. The civil war is another weight preventing it from moving forward.

Understanding Syria

The modern-day country of Syria is considered part of the Middle East. It is bordered to the north by Turkey, the south by Jordan, and the east by Iraq. The nation's western border stretches along the Mediterranean Sea, facing the island nation of Cyprus. That border is interrupted only by a short section of Israel and the tiny country of Lebanon, which sits along Syria's southeast boundary. Syria itself is small, about the size of the state of Washington. Its Mediterranean Sea coastline, a mix of sandy bays and rocky cliffs, is only 110 miles (180 kilometers).

A Land of Black Blizzards

Most of the country is flat plains (steppe), and most of that is the Syrian Desert. It is not a sand desert; it is rock and gravel. Still, dust storms whip across it frequently. Wind moving at as little as 9 miles (14.5 km) an hour can kick up dirt from the ground. With a little more force, as well as the right meteorological conditions, a dark wall of dust

People walking in the town of Bukamal, Syria, near the border with Iraq, are difficult to see because of a sandstorm.

can rise and move. This kind of storm is often referred to as a "black blizzard."

These storms can be huge, unstoppable forces of nature. They can move at hurricane speeds for up to fifty days. In the sixth century BCE in Egypt, not far from present-day Syria, an army of fifty thousand soldiers was buried by a dust storm. In Arabic, the word for one such intense storm is "haboob," after the strong wind that causes it.

Agriculture in a Desert

Less than 10 percent of Syria is arable, or able to be farmed. Yet agriculture plays an important role in the country's economy; it amounts to 20 percent of the national income. Syria gets most of its rain in the winter, which does crops little good. Rising temperatures are lessening the already low amount of rain the country gets. Farmers must rely on irrigation, directing water themselves to their crops. The water they use is usually from aquifers, permeable rock that holds water. These porous rocks, mostly sandstone and chalk and some basalt and limestone, cover half the country. Rainwater seeps through these rocky layers and forms underground springs. Unfortunately for these farmers, these underground pockets of water are so close to the surface that they can dry up.

Syria has rivers, but those don't help to irrigate the farmland. The Euphrates River is the country's most important aboveground water source. However, Turkey, where it originates, and Iraq both also draw heavily on it, leaving Syria with too little. The Orontes River is Syria's high-altitude water source. It starts in Lebanon and flows north through Syria's mountains. The Baradā River flows through the capital city of Damascus.

The Mountains

Syria's four main areas of settlement, where humans live, are the coast, the farmland, the desert, and the mountains. The country's plains are studded with mountains. The Al-Anṣariyyah mountain range borders the coast, running north and south. Its highest point is just over 5,000 feet (1,562 meters). The Anti-Lebanon Mountains run between Syria and Lebanon. They include Syria's tallest mountain,

Mount Hermon. It is 9,232 feet (2,814 m). The country's only forests are in the Al-Anṣariyyah. Because there's little work in the mountains, people have been moving to the steppe and the coast.

The Oldest Cities in the World

Syria is home to two of the oldest urban centers in the world. For a long time, Damascus, the country's capital, was considered the world's oldest city. But evidence of a settlement dating to 9000 BCE has been found only *near* the present-day city, not technically within its borders. Damascus proper seems to have been founded around 2000 BCE.

Aleppo, north of Damascus, used to be the country's largest city. Since the country's violent civil unrest began in 2011, Aleppo is now second in population to the capital. It maintains its storied history, however. Written records indicate it was always, until recently, the country's most important city. Once a formidable rival to the historically powerhouse cities of Cairo, Egypt; and Constantinople (now Istanbul), Turkey; Aleppo has existed as a settlement since 6000 BCE. Depending on the definition of "city," some view Aleppo as tracing back to much earlier than that even. Some people say areas have to trade with other places to be considered cities; others say there must be available services such as plumbing. According to a looser definition of "city,"

ABU BAKR AL-BAGHDADI: THE LEADER OF ISIS

ISIS, ISIL, and IS are all names for the Islamic State terrorist organization, a deadly actor in the Syrian Civil War. Daesh is also a name for the group, though it's not one that the group itself uses. It is an acronym formed with the first letters of the group's original name: "al-Dawla al-Islamiya fil Iraq wa al-Sham." Just as English-speaking governments and media use many different names for the terrorist group, its leader has disguised his identity with many names.

Abu Bakr al-Baghdadi has been ISIS's leader since 2010—or he was its leader. He may be dead or in hiding. In February 2018, it was reported that he was severely wounded in an attack. He survived, but it was not known if he was still running ISIS. In fact, his nickname is "the invisible sheikh." Furthermore, no one knows his real name. (Baghdadi is a cover name.) Because of this, it is difficult to know much about his present, let alone his past. It's believed he was born in 1971 in Samarra, north of Baghdad, Iraq. He may have been a cleric during the US-led invasion of that city in 2003. He may have always been a militant, or he may have been radicalized during his four-year detainment at Camp Bucca, a US facility in southern Iraq. No matter his biographical details, he has had a terrible impact on the world.

Aleppo has been one since around 11,000 BCE. That's when nomads set up temporary camps there. Its citadel, developed in the third century BCE, became one of the region's most impressive military fortresses. Hundreds of years later, in present day, it became the only ancient citadel to be used as a modern garrison and artillery battery.

Homs, Syria's third-largest city, has existed only since the first millennium BCE, but even this "youthful" city has made a major mark on the world. During the Roman era, when it was known as Emesa, it was an important trading post between India and China and the Mediterranean. Today, it's Syria's industrial center; it is both a road and rail hub and home to the country's largest oil refinery. It has also been called, since 2011, the "capital of the revolution."

The Many Faces of War

Though Syria's war started as two-sided, the citizens versus the government, it is now a tangle of opposition forces. Three of the main players are the government, ISIS, and al-Qaeda. All three have involved teenagers in their activities—as soldiers, as hostages, or both.

President Bashar al-Assad's side has not only the power of the national military behind it, including an air force, but also the support of a world power: Russia. Russia has funded Assad's efforts with the equivalent of billions of American

Syrian President
Bashar al-Assad

dollars. As an Alawite Muslim, which is related to Shiism, Assad is also supported by Shiite Iran. Along with Iran's money and soldiers come its allies, like Hezbollah, a militant group from Lebanon.

ISIS, on the other hand, stands for the "Islamic State of Iraq and Syria." Working within the chaos of Syria's war, this terrorist group has increased its power. It started as an al-Qaeda affiliate but split from that group in 2013.

Then there is al-Qaeda's continued presence in Syria. Until 2016, al-Qaeda's Syrian-based affiliate was known as Jabhat al-Nusra. CNN called this group "the most deadly" of groups in the Syrian Civil War. In 2016, Jabhat al-Nusra claimed to separate from al-Qaeda. The group then changed its name to Jabhat Fateh al-Sham and later changed its name again, this time to Hayat Tahrir al-Sham (HTS). Many experts say that claiming to separate from al-Qaeda was a strategic move. These experts believe HTS remains part of al-Qaeda. Others think the split is genuine. ISIS may make headlines, but HTS is building relationships within the country, converting civilians and opposition groups to its side.

THE GLOBAL COALITION

Terrorist groups aren't the only groups making gains in Syria. The Global Coalition is an international group working to defeat ISIS. The United States started the coalition. As of early 2018, seventy-three nations and organizations, like the European Union, NATO, and Interpol, had signed on as partners.

The Global Coalition's goals include the following:

Participating in a military campaign in Iraq and Syria.
According to the coalition's website, as of early 2018, it had helped local groups push ISIS out of 95 percent of the territory it had controlled.

Destroying ISIS's finances and dismantling its economic structure.
Working together, the Global Coalition's members, which are spread around the globe, have prevented ISIS from moving money or doing business in many places. Where ISIS has taken control of a country's resources, such as its oil fields or transportation assets, the coalition targets air strikes accordingly to drive ISIS away and return the resources to the country.

Preventing fighters from other countries from joining ISIS.
The Counter-Daesh Coalition Working Group on Foreign Terrorist Fighters helps countries follow a United Nations Security Council resolution from 2014. Resolution 2178 requires countries to crack down on foreign terrorist fighters.

Supporting areas liberated from ISIS.
As of late 2017, the coalition had pledged more than $50 million to the United Nations Development Program's (UNDP) Funding Facility for Immediate Stabilization (FFIS). The FFIS helps people who fled their homes return and rebuild.

Generally "exposing [ISIS's] delusional narrative."
ISIS is skillful at manipulating social media to explain its message to prospective recruits, inspire its allies, and scare its enemies. The Global Coalition produces messages counter to ISIS's. It also assists and boosts other voices from the region.

Palmyra, northeast of modern-day Damascus, was one of the world's most important cultural centers in the first and second centuries.

CHAPTER TWO

A CONFLICT CENTURIES IN THE MAKING

Terrorist organizations thrive during times of chaos, and much of Syria's history involves instability. Its borders have changed, and its rulers have changed. Its harsh natural environment has added more challenges. The terrorist groups participating in today's Syrian Civil War rose to power thanks to a power vacuum thousands of years old.

This does not mean Syria is a place without beauty and accomplishment. There are many examples of its importance in the world. Prior to the onset of the civil war, the nation's vibrant cities and towns brought visitors from around the world. Bones from some of the earliest humans have been found there, and Syria is mentioned often in the Bible. At the same time, occupation is not new to Syrians. Many groups have occupied and ruled the nation over the centuries.

The Many Rulers of Ancient Syria

Throughout ancient times, Syria was occupied by the Egyptians, Hittites, Sumerians, Mitanni, Assyrians, Babylonians, Canaanites, Phoenicians, Arameans, Amorites, Persians, Greeks, and Romans, among others. When the Roman Empire fell, the Byzantine Empire replaced it.

In the early seventh century CE, the prophet Muhammad started Islam. The new religion began to take hold in many places. Syria first became an Islamic state in 637 CE, when Muslim forces defeated the Byzantines. For a time, Damascus was the capital of the Islamic world.

In 1516, the Ottoman Empire conquered Syria. For 402 years, the country remained a part of the empire. In many ways, there was stability. The government kept order but also allowed for people to lead their lives as they wanted.

However, by the beginning of the 1800s, the country would face new clashes. Egyptian forces began to occupy Syria in 1831. In turn, Egyptian occupation led to European involvement in Syria. In 1840, Britain encouraged the Syrian citizens to rebel against the Egyptians. This was the beginning of the end of the Ottoman Empire too. It was also the beginning of long-standing Western involvement in the country.

European Control and Semi-autonomy

In the early twentieth century, the Ottoman Empire found itself on the losing side of World War I. Britain and France

The Great Mosque of Damascus, also called the Umayyad Mosque, is the world's oldest stone mosque, built in the eighth century CE.

divided most of what we now know as the Middle East between them. From 1918 to 1920, Damascus and Aleppo were under British control. The French took control of the whole country in 1920. Soon after, Syrians rose against their colonial rulers. The Syrian Revolt lasted from 1925 to 1927. It took until 1936 for France and Syria to negotiate a solution both countries found acceptable. France would maintain military and economic control. In other ways, Syria would be considered independent. After ten more years and another world war, during which both British and French troops occupied Syria, the country would become fully independent.

The Lasting Consequences of French Rule

Today's Syrians come from diverse racial, ethnic, and religious backgrounds. Considering all the different ruling groups the area has had over thousands of years, this is not surprising. When those groups moved in and occupied Syria, they brought their ideas and also some of their own citizens. They mixed with the people already living in Syria. This created a cultural hotspot.

The diversity was not discouraged. According to an article in the *Atlantic*, "Syria also has historically been a sanctuary for little groups of peoples whose differences from one another were defined in religious and/or ethnic terms." During Ottoman rule, people did not consider themselves part of a nation-state called Syria. They were part of an empire. They could move from one part of it to the other "without feeling or being considered alien." Syria is majority Muslim, and has been for centuries, but there were still examples of religious tolerance. First, there is more than one sect within Islam. Today, conflict among these branches has caused wars. Back then, the groups lived peacefully together. Second, even non-Muslim communities in Syria maintained their unique languages and customs. They paid taxes to the empire, but they also elected their own local leaders and ran their own schools.

France claiming Syria from the Ottomans after World War I changed all of that for the worse. The European country began cutting Syria into pieces. The pieces weren't given equal consideration. One, for example, was made its own nation. Another remained a French colony but was also autonomous. Another was even given away, to Turkey. The French made both Damascus and Aleppo capital cities.

Unsurprisingly, that didn't make people happy. The French reunited the pieces and tried changing the national language from Arabic to French. They also tried to change the national religion from Islam to Catholicism. France sent forces to Damascus no fewer than three times and established martial law during "peaceful" times. The French handed down constitutions to the Syrians and then canceled them. As the *Atlantic* article explained, the French did not create all internal disagreements among Syrian groups, but they "certainly magnified" them.

The Early Decades of "Independence"

Tragically, modern Syria has never gotten to enjoy full independence. A series of government coups followed the country's release from France. Different people tried to claim control of the new nation. Eventually, looking for stability, Syria joined with Egypt to become the United Arab Republic. That unification started in 1958 and ended in 1961.

Syria's neighbors' struggles affected Syria too. Syria was not the only Middle Eastern country to be "created" after World War II. Israel was formed as a new Jewish state. Just as Syria struggled with its new role in the world, so too did Israel. The Six-Day War of 1967 pitted Israel against the region's other countries. On April 7, Israel seized the Golan Heights, a rocky plateau along Syria's southwestern border with Israel. Israel continues to control the area. In 1973, Syria went to full war with Israel.

Syrians vs. Syrians

Attacked regularly by outside forces, Syria also has a bloody history of infighting. Hafiz al-Assad, who was president of Syria from 1970 until his death thirty years later, ruled the country as an Alawite. That is a minority Shiite sect. In 1982, the Muslim Brotherhood (of the Sunni sect), organized a rebellion against Assad. The president had the rebels arrested, tortured, and eventually executed. The government's retaliation stretched wide, and many experts think about twenty thousand civilians ended up dying because of it.

In 2000, Bashar al-Assad became president after his father's death. He seemed at first to be more tolerant of political dissidents than his father. He released six hundred political prisoners. Within a year, though, he was threatening anyone who spoke out against his administration. Syria became known as a place where people who disagreed with the government were not safe.

Arab Spring

The Arab Spring revolts in Egypt and Tunisia in early 2011 are considered directly related to Syria's civil war. Revolution was in the air. That revolution started in a horrifying way in Tunisia.

SONGS OF HOME

In 2012, a girl named Fatmeh could see the whole world spread before her. She was just about to turn thirteen. She lived with her parents and siblings in a big house in Syria. Her mother tended to the garden while her father taught high school geography, sociology, and health. Fatmeh herself was on the track to college. She particularly loved her Arabic literature classes.

Refugees from Syria now live in Beqaa Valley, Lebanon (pictured here).

At the same time, the Syrian Civil War edged closer to Fatmeh's town. The fighting was no longer just something on the news. "Bombs and fighting were everywhere," Fatmeh told NPR's *All Things Considered*. "We lost a neighbor, a cousin, and the husband of our aunt. The house next to ours was bombed. So we left to survive."

They walked for a day. Fatmeh and her older sister sometimes carried their younger siblings. The next day, a truck stopped to help them. They stood crowded on the back of it until they arrived in Lebanon's Beqaa Valley. Just like Fatmeh's home used to be in an idyllic setting, the valley had been Lebanon's farmland and wine country. By the time Fatmeh's family arrived, it had become home to hundreds of thousands of refugees from Syria.

When NPR interviewed her, Fatmeh had been a refugee for three years. She could not go to school. Instead, she had to work in the fields. In her few hours of downtime each day, she was on her cell phone. She read news about Syria. If she found some privacy, she recorded herself singing songs about her home.

On December 17, 2010, police confiscated the fruits and vegetables of a twenty-seven-year-old street vendor. They said he didn't have a permit to sell. If the vendor had paid the police a bribe, they may have given him back his products and let him continue to sell them. However, he did not have money for a bribe. He was tired of police harassment too. In protest, he killed himself outside the governor's office.

The bold action of one person encouraged people in Tunisia, and then across the Middle East, to protest en masse. Citizens marched in the streets. They were tired of the corruption and abuse of power in their governments. What happened in Egypt and Tunisia inspired citizens and worried government leaders. It was only a matter of time before Syria saw conflict.

Environmental Reasons for the Syrian War

War, occupation, and political oppression were not the only factors that made Syria vulnerable to terrorist organizations. From 2001 to 2010, sixty massive dust storms battered Syria. In the five years leading up to the Syrian Civil War, the country experienced a severe drought. All of this contributed to the civil war starting.

Dust storms and droughts have a history of causing social and political disruption around the world. For example, during the Dust Bowl of 1930s America, hundreds of thousands of people were displaced. They were forced to leave their homes in Oklahoma, Texas, Kansas, and Nebraska.

Dust storms also can cause health problems. By kicking particles into the air, they leave people breathing mold, heavy

Sheep look for grass to eat in Hasaka, Syria, during a drought.

metals from pollutants, and diseases. Dust storms have even been linked to meningitis in northern Africa. Contaminants found in the dust in Kuwait and Iraq may be a cause of Gulf War syndrome, a cluster of illnesses that veterans experienced after Operation Desert Storm in the 1990s. In August and September 2015, a major dust storm covered Syria, as well as Lebanon, Turkey, Israel, Egypt, Jordan, and Palestine. The air was so thick with sand that the region could not be seen in images from satellites. At times, the particles in the air were bigger than any measured since 1995. Thousands of people experienced problems breathing, and some even died.

For a long time, the Syrian Civil War was blamed for starting the storm. The increased number of soldiers and military vehicles traveling over unpaved roads had loosened the dirt. Farmers had been forced to abandon their fields because of the fighting, so there were no crops to hold the earth together or keep it from eroding. In early 2017, researchers suggested a different cause. The summer of 2015 had been unusually hot and dry, so dirt was looser than usual, not as wet and packed down. When wind hit, there was more dust to stir up.

Environmental factors stretch beyond storms, though. *Smithsonian* magazine reported that the first documented war caused by water happened 4,500 years ago—where modern-day Syria sits today. The connection between lack of water and increased violence seems to continue today. In 2013, the Gravity Recovery and Climate Experiment (GRACE), showed that Turkey, Syria, Iraq, and western Iran were losing water faster than almost any other place in the world. "While the scientists captured dropping water levels," according to *Smithsonian*, "political experts have observed rising tensions."

This includes rising conflict in Syria and between Syria and its neighbors. The 2006–2011 drought forced many farmers to migrate to cities to look for work. They could no longer make a living growing crops in completely parched earth. "There's some evidence that the migration fueled the civil war there," one water management expert told the magazine. "You had a lot of angry, unemployed men helping to trigger a revolution." Syria also has accused neighbor Turkey of hoarding water. Turkey's dam and hydropower construction along the region's shared waterways resulted in 40 percent less water than usual reaching Syria.

A Complicated War

There are not just two groups fighting in the Syrian Civil War. In reality, the war is a complex web of fighting. Sometimes a few groups join together to fight a common enemy; sometimes they battle each other. The two primary two sides are "the government" and "those opposing the government." Yet there is more than one group on each side, and sometimes they disagree with each other.

The Assad administration has the support of Syria's military; the Alawites, people who follow that sect of Islam; Hezbollah, a group based out of Lebanon, which the United States considers a terrorist group; Russia; and Iran. The opposition side has the support of Saudi Arabia, Qatar, Turkey, Jordan, and the Sunnis (people who follow that unique branch of Islam). It is also supported by several other groups, according to a 2016 article published in *Globalo*. Some of these groups formed long before the Syrian Civil War. They have goals outside of Syria, but they are also fighting in this war because they recognize the importance of Syria in the region. Many of these groups formed only once the war started.

The Free Syrian Army (FSA) is one such group. One hundred thousand deserters from the Syrian Armed Forces have claimed to want to take down the Assad government. The United States has trained the FSA and provided the soldiers with weapons. The Global Coalition, which is a group of countries and organizations fighting ISIS, may have also assisted the FSA.

Asala wa-al-Tanmiya is supported by the United States too. As of 2016, Asala wa-al-Tanmiya had thirteen thousand soldiers. The United States seized American-made

BGM-71 TOW weapons from ISIS and gave them to this group. Saudi Arabia also contributes support to Asala wa-al-Tanmiya, which is also known as the Authenticity and Development Front.

In addition to the Authenticity and Development Front, Saudi Arabia backs Jaish al-Fatah. These ten thousand soldiers are primarily opposed to the Assad government but aren't necessarily against ISIS. Turkey is another supporter.

Yet another group is Harakat Ahrar ash-Sham al-Islamiyya. At ten thousand to twenty thousand soldiers, Ahrar ash-Sham is the largest rebel group in Syria. These people fight primarily against the Assad government. They also want to create an Islamic state that follows sharia law. The United States thinks they are aligned with al-Qaeda. Turkey and Saudi Arabia support the group.

As of 2016, a faction called the Sham Legion had about four thousand soldiers. It is a union of moderate Islamist rebel groups. The Ajnad al-Sham Islamic Union is a similar size; around three thousand soldiers are part of this collective of Islamist groups. Like several of the groups fighting, it formed in response to the Syrian Civil War.

Then there is the largest rebel faction in Damascus, Jaysh al-Islam. These seventeen thousand to twenty-five thousand soldiers were also known as Liwa al-Islam or the Brigade of Islam. The group wanted to create an Islamic state that

FREECOM

Twenty-seven-year-old software engineer Abdul Rahman al-Ashraf was the European Youth digital champion for 2016 for an app he developed to help people living in war zones. Though he had moved to Germany to complete his master's degree, Abdul grew up in Syria and used his experiences living through its civil war to create the app, called FreeCom.

A Syrian woman uses her cell phone at Jordan's Zaatari refugee camp, which was home to eighty thousand Syrian refugees by 2017.

FreeCom is a free communication tool that allows people to use their smart phones even when internet connections or mobile network signals are unavailable. Also, messages sent through the app are encrypted. That means third parties can't spy on FreeCom communications.

According to Abdul in his 2017 TEDxMünster talk, seventeen countries were experiencing disruptive conflicts or wars that year. Around 60 percent of the world's population didn't have reliable internet access. He said that one of his "biggest fears" during the Syrian Civil War was "being disconnected and isolated from the whole world for days, weeks, sometimes for months." He experienced this firsthand when an area only 6 miles (10 km) from where he was living in Damascus was disconnected for five months. Every day, he checked for messages from friends and family. He was desperate to know if they were all right. To not hear from them for so long was "one of the hardest experiences in my life," he said.

The European Youth Award is an annual contest that asks young people to create digital projects that are socially valuable. Abdul hopes that the app will be made available for people living in war zones and natural disaster areas. He imagines its applications will grow beyond war to meet the needs of people anywhere internet signal is weak.

follows sharia law. Syria, Russia, Iran, and Egypt have called it a terrorist organization. All told, experts say there are more than one hundred factions involved in the war in Syria.

Child Soldiers on All Sides

In 2016, United Press International (UPI) published an article about child soldiers in the Syrian Civil War. "Militarizing children has become common in the Syrian war," said the article, "with all sides guilty of what is considered a war crime in international law." It based this statement on interviews with child soldiers and military leaders conducted by the Syrian Independent Media Group.

Even though some groups will not allow interviews with their soldiers, other sources have confirmed the use of child soldiers in all groups, even though who claim not to use them. Civilians have said Jabhat al-Nusra patrolled their neighborhoods to enlist children. In 2014, Human Rights Watch found that al-Nusra "[required] its child soldiers to sign documents agreeing to participate in suicide missions." The Syrian government ratified the UN's protocol for protecting children's rights, meaning it pledged not to recruit young people for its military. This promise does not cover groups directly assisting the military.

The Rise of Teen Soldiers in Syria

Syria has long been a place many people have wanted to live. Some of those settlements have been made peacefully. In many other cases, groups have violently forced themselves onto the land. Because of this, the area, now an independent country, is home to diverse people and cultures. Each have their own goals, enemies, and allies. Syria's neighboring countries also have rich, complicated histories. Their agreements and disagreements easily affect Syria as well. Add in the country's rough terrain and extreme weather, and tension can easily spark into fighting—among not just two groups but many. That is what happened in Syria in 2011, when the civil war started.

As the fighting stretched on for years, more and more young people became involved. Some had lost parents, so they had no adults to care for them. Many were forced out of their homes and could no longer attend school. All questioned what their futures looked like. They might join military groups out of desperation. Those groups welcomed them and sometimes even forced them to join because the soldiers were desperate too. The longer a war lasts, the more people are needed to fight. Many teens in Syria have become military recruits in the Syrian Civil War.

A child soldier fights for the Free Syrian Army in 2013 in Aleppo, Syria.

CHAPTER THREE

TEEN RECRUITS

UNICEF, the children's relief organization, declared 2016 to be the worst year yet for Syria's children. That year, 851 young people were recruited as child soldiers. That number was double what it was in 2015. No one knows how many teen soldiers have fought in the Syrian Civil War overall. There are too many groups fighting to accurately monitor. Some groups refuse any access to their soldiers. Experts do know that all militaries in Syria are using child soldiers. Human Rights Watch has studied the use of child soldiers in nonstate, armed groups in Syria. The United Nations International Commission of Inquiry has documented pro-Assad troops using them. Some of the young people even fight with two or three armed groups.

Some teen soldiers are spies. Some act as basic medics, treating battlefield wounds. Some are couriers, carrying ammunition and other supplies. Some are made to be "brides" to male soldiers and must bear their children. Some fight as snipers or right on the front lines. The Violations Documenting Center, a group out of Syria, documented the deaths of 194 "noncivilian" male children between September 2011 and May 2014.

By international law, it is a war crime for militaries or any armed groups to recruit and use children in any way. The Optional Protocol to the United Nations Convention on the Rights of the Child (UNCRC) bans nonstate armies from using children. Syria ratified, or agreed to, that ban in 2003. According to the UNCRC, all children have rights to develop physically and mentally to their fullest (article 6), to receive health care (article 24), to be protected from violence (article 19) and armed conflict (article 38), and to have access to education (article 28). If a child or teen is part of a military, that person's rights are being violated.

Some armed groups have told Human Rights Watch that they don't officially accept soldiers who are younger than eighteen. However, they will accept teens if the kids approach them. "Sixteen, seventeen is not young. [If we don't take him,] he'll go fight on his own," said Abu Rida, leader of one of the Free Syrian Army brigades.

Zama Coursen-Neff, the head of the children's rights division of Human Rights Watch ,spoke with *Time* magazine in 2014 about the organization's report on child soldiers in Syria. She said that extremist groups "aggressively targeted" children to join them as soldiers. "It's bad enough that the Syrian government is dropping bombs on children," Coursen-Neff told the magazine. "Armed opposition groups in Syria should not in turn be sending children into harm's way."

Recruiting the Desperate

In 2016, the *Christian Science Monitor* reported on a new, very effective ISIS recruiting strategy. It was using its incredible budget to promise money and resources to the poorest of people.

According to *Business Insider*, ISIS had $1 billion in revenue in 2015. It got money from trading oil and taxing the residents of the territories it captured. It then started putting that money toward salaries and gifts.

"Children report being actively encouraged to join the war by parties to the conflict offering gifts and 'salaries' of up to $400 a month," UNICEF said in 2016, as reported by Reuters. Interestingly, *Business Insider* reported, fighter salaries varied depending on where they came from. Syrian ISIS militants received about $200 per month, not the $400 that those from some other countries received. According to

United Press International (UPI) in 2016, teens fighting for ISIS may get $65 per month. Their parents receive a "health basket" of food. Child soldiers fighting on the front line for the FSA received $30–$35 every once in a while. Any amount is often still a big deal to a lot of teens and their families. "The salary is still a deciding factor for those that are desperate for a source of income," wrote the *Business Insider*.

Time magazine reported on Majed, who was a sixteen-year-old living in southwestern Syria when the civil war started. He helped his family by farming tomatoes. Then one of the rebel groups, al-Nusra, took over his town. Majed was attracted to what the soldiers were offering. They gave him rides in cars. They taught reading and how to use a gun. They gave rewards for good marksmanship.

"Thousands of families in impoverished neighborhoods are suddenly living beyond their means, and it is all because their sons are fighting in Syria and Iraq," Badra Gaaloul, president of the International Centre for Strategic, Security and Military Studies, told the *Christian Science Monitor*.

Extremist groups also appeal to teens who are bored. If their schools have been bombed, they do not have much to do with their days.

Abu Yahya, a leader of Jaish al-Sham fighting in Syria, told UPI, "There are no schools or anything like that around here … [Teens] come in and ask us to make them soldiers."

The Syrian military bombed this school in 2016.

Mahmoud al-Abbas was a sixteen-year-old when he enlisted with Ahrar al-Sham. "I asked where I could find the headquarters of the fighting groups for the opposition," he told UPI. "Of course, there are financial reasons behind why I chose to fight, plus there are no schools to study in, there is no work."

Recruiting the Lonely

When Alex (her online name) was born, her mom was struggling with drug and alcohol addiction. Her father was not in the picture. Before Alex was even a year old, her mother had lost custody of her. Alex was fortunate that her grandparents could take her in.

They lived in rural Washington State. To get to their home from the nearest town, you turned at the trailer park and drove a mile through wheat and alfalfa fields. "My grandparents enjoy living in the middle of nowhere," Alex told the *New York Times*. "I enjoy community. It gets lonely here."

The newspaper conducted an in-depth interview with her and her family in 2015. This was a "rare window into the intense effort to indoctrinate a young American woman" by a foreign terrorist organization. In this case, that organization was ISIS.

Why ISIS Was Interested in Alex

There was one factor in particular that made Alex a strong possible recruit: she was a Westerner. Americans, Canadians, Europeans, and Australians have "outside propaganda value," the *New York Times* explained. They get a lot of attention from the media. One of ISIS's terror techniques has always been to heavily use social media. It is known for blasting Twitter with videos of its actions. It then relies on people, including the media, to retweet those images and to talk about them. When ISIS got involved in the Syrian Civil War, it found another reason it needed Westerners. It needed people who attracted media attention to encourage recruitment. "Once ISIS expanded into Syria, it was forced to compete with a lot of jihadi groups," Laith Alkhouri told the *New York*

Times. Alkhouri is an analyst who tracked the websites of militant groups. "It literally revolutionized how it produced, distributed, and translated its message very quickly."

Alex was also attractive to ISIS because she was a person of religious faith. Though she was a Christian, not a Muslim, she had been thinking about adhering to faith more fully. ISIS uses that interest in religion, any religion, to win over possible recruits. Because ISIS began as a partner organization to al-Qaeda, ISIS members follow some al-Qaeda recruitment tactics. Al-Qaeda published a manual called *A Course in the Art of Recruiting.* ISIS members still employ the manual's recommendations. One of the recommendations is to "start with the religious rituals [of Islam] and concentrate on them." ISIS tries to persuade people by claiming to be just a deeply religious organization. It also does not place itself in full opposition to Christianity. One of Alex's ISIS "friends" sent her this message once: "What you do not know is that I am not inviting you to leave Christianity. Islam is the correction of Christianity."

Alex also thought she had few job prospects in rural Washington. She had dropped out of college. She worked for a year at a day care and then resigned. She tried working at a customer-support call center. She quit after three weeks of training. She earned $300 a month babysitting and teaching Sunday school. Alex later told the *New York Times* that she liked following the guidance of the ISIS supporters she met online. It gave her a sense of purpose.

Perhaps most of all, she was lonely. ISIS seemed to be a friend. Like so many young people, she spent a lot of her free time on social media. She lived in a tiny community, so the internet was her main connection to the world.

Alex's First ISIS "Friend"

One day, Alex read about ISIS killing an American journalist. She had never heard of the group. The story was so shocking that she could not stop thinking about it. She went online to learn more. She decided to try to find people who agreed with the journalist's captors to understand why they had killed the man.

Alex easily found ISIS supporters on Twitter. They "politely" answered her questions. "Once they saw that I was sincere in my curiosity, they were very kind," she said. Then they started asking her questions. They wondered about her family. They asked what her goals in life were.

Her first ISIS "friend" was Monzer Hamad. He was fighting in the Syrian Civil War, near Damascus. They chatted online for hours every day. Alex shared these messages with the *New York Times*. They were filled with emojis and LOLs. They talked about gardening and food.

ISIS members are trained to be friendly with possible recruits. They are trained to be good listeners and to demonstrate empathy. In this way, they seem to be a friend. The person they are targeting trusts them more and more. Soon, that person might do what the ISIS members ask them to do.

Alex often spent time alone, but ISIS was always online. Her real-life friends never answered her messages as quickly as Hamad and the others did. Alex's pastor at church also did not answer her questions about God and religion the way Hamad did. Hamad seemed knowledgeable about the Bible. He also always had time for Alex's questions. Alex had a different experience when she tried to talk with her pastor. She asked difficult questions about Christianity. Her pastor told her "she needed to trust in the mystery of God." He ended their meeting after fifteen minutes.

Alex Converts to Islam

Alex connected with another ISIS supporter online. She and Faisal Mostafa started Skyping for hours every day. They kept the cameras turned off. They talked sometimes for seven hours in one stretch. He guided her through Muslim rituals. Sometimes, he connected what they did to Bible verses.

Finally, Alex believed in her heart that she was no longer practicing her Christian faith. She asked Mostafa how to convert to Islam. He told her to declare her belief in Allah in front of two Muslims. She did not know any in real life. He told her to post online. There were lots of witnesses there.

One night, while her family watched television, completely unaware who Alex had been talking to for months, Alex committed to Islam on Twitter. She was overwhelmed by making this major life change. She explained that converting was such a big deal to her that she worried she might get sick. That anxiety quickly passed. Alex was overjoyed as she watched her Twitter following double. She believed she was making meaningful connections.

Alex began receiving presents in the mail from her ISIS "friends." They sent her hijabs, prayer rugs, and books. Alex told just one real-life person, her cousin, about her conversations and conversion. After that, she received an envelope from overseas. Inside was a greeting card decorated with a kitten. Inside that were two $20 bills. The note read, "Please go out and enjoy a pizza TOGETHER."

More Isolation

Alex did some research and found a mosque only 5 miles (8 km) from her home. She was excited that she could finally be among her new community in real life. However, her ISIS "friends" rushed to tell her she shouldn't try to visit it. Muslims were persecuted in the United States, they said, so

REPLY-ALL TERRORISM

According to an article reprinted in the *Atlantic* in 2015, by that year ISIS recruitment in the United States was at an "unprecedented" level. ISIS was reaching Americans far more quickly and efficiently than al-Qaeda, its onetime affiliate, ever did.

In October 2015, US authorities were actively investigating 900 American ISIS sympathizers. These people lived in all fifty states and came from all walks of life. At least 250 other Americans traveled or tried to travel to Syria or Iraq to join ISIS.

Analysts at the George Washington University Program on Extremism spent six months monitoring American ISIS supporters. They found that most of these American recruits came to ISIS through social media networks such as Twitter and Instagram. Many wanted a sense of community and personal identity by joining ISIS.

Though ISIS follows the recommendations in the al-Qaeda recruitment manual *A Course in the Art of Recruiting*, the organization has found a new medium for its tactics: the internet. ISIS members and supporters are online twenty-four hours a day. They reply quickly to messages. They patiently build relationships with prospective recruits. In some circumstances, they spend thousands of hours over the course of months laying the groundwork for recruitment.

she might be labeled a terrorist. Alex kept teaching Sunday school, but she listened to ISIS anthems on her phone while she drove there. At church, she bowed her head with everyone else, but she said different prayers in her mind.

ISIS was not trying to protect her from harm. Its supporters were trying to keep her from discovering their lies. If she had gone to the mosque, she would have learned that her ISIS contacts were not teaching her about true Islam. Also, by keeping her from real-life friends, they could foster her isolation. She would continue to feel connected only to them.

Mubin Shaikh used to be a recruiter for an extremist Islamist group. He told the *New York Times* what he used to do: "We look for people who are isolated. And if they are not isolated already, then we isolated them."

Shaikh was, in fact, someone who tried to help Alex. Some of her conversations with ISIS were happening publicly on Twitter. Shaikh wrote to her to stop. Others did too. Someone who went by the handle, or online name, KindLadyAdilah tweeted a warning to Alex. KindLadyAdilah said that Alex was in danger and could die if she went abroad. KindLadyAdilah tried to make Alex see reason.

Alex's ISIS connections started demanding she stop talking with people who were "kuffar," or infidels. This included people trying to help her online as well as her Christian friends. Someone accused her of being a spy against the Islamic State. People Alex thought were her friends blocked her online.

Alex immediately sent a public message offering to give her Twitter password to anyone who wanted to review her private messages. She wrote that she had nothing to hide. Alex said that her conversion felt like it saved her life. She wanted people to stop accusing her of being a spy. The offer to share her password was meant to prove her faith was strong and real. Mostafa stepped in and smoothed things over. He then assured Alex, saying that he knew she was a true believer and that he knew it would be easy for her to find a husband.

Next Steps

Alex's last romantic relationship had ended years before. Just like she did not see a career for herself in rural Washington, she could not imagine finding someone to marry there, either. She began daydreaming about being a mother for the Islamic State. Mostafa suggested she meet him where he lived, Austria. He would introduce her to the man he had in mind to be her husband. Perhaps from there, they would travel to "a Muslim land." Alex guessed he meant Syria.

Mostafa and the others had not shied away from talking about violence with Alex. They downplayed the killings Alex saw on television. She started to believe that what the media said about ISIS was not true. She spent Valentine's Day that year chatting with an ISIS supporter whose handle was SurgeonOf Death. Mostafa always included Lindt chocolate bars in his packages to her. He did so because he admired the man who, earlier that year, had held hostages in the name of ISIS at an Australian Lindt café.

Real-Life Intervention

Alex's grandmother finally caught on that something bad was happening with her granddaughter. Alex had been sneaky with her communications. She even borrowed phones and computers when her grandmother took hers away. Still, her grandmother persisted. One day, she contacted Mostafa.

Alex's grandmother told Mostafa how much Alex meant to her family. She emphasized that there was no way they would allow Alex to go abroad to join a terrorist organization like ISIS.

Mostafa replied, saying that he knew Alex's grandmother thought that he was a radical Muslim. He claimed that Alex's grandmother didn't have the full story. Mostafa said that he did not support terrorism or violence. Furthermore, he said that he would never put Alex in a dangerous situation.

People created a memorial at the Lindt Café in Sydney, Australia, following an attack by an ISIS follower. Alex's ISIS contact admired him.

Alex's grandmother continued the conversation briefly. She never backed down. Mostafa finally agreed not to contact Alex again. Alex agreed to give her grandmother control of her online accounts. They contacted the Federal Bureau of Investigation (FBI). The FBI downloaded all of Alex's communications with ISIS.

ISIS has been so successful at recruiting people in large part because it never gives up. Supporters are willing to spend a lot of time with potential converts. They do this so that those people will want to then do whatever the supporters ask of them. This is called grooming. Even after the FBI got involved in Alex's case, Alex could not forget about the ISIS supporters she had met online. She figured out a way to contact Mostafa again. He wrote her back immediately. "I told [your grandmother] I would not communicate with you," he typed. "But I lied."

Recruiting the Angry

According to Human Rights Watch, boys in Syria join armed groups for several different reasons. Some tag along with friends or relatives. Some have nothing else to do because their schools have been destroyed. Some are trying to provide for their starving families; some teen soldiers are paid to fight—or are promised payment. Some are angry and truly believe they want to go to battle. They may have lost loved ones to the war and want revenge. Human Rights Watch reported that few had dreams for the future. "Maybe we'll live, and maybe we'll die," said Omar, who became a soldier at age fourteen with Jabhat al-Nusra. This attitude is in stark contrast with that of teens who are not soldiers. In studies of Syrian teens who are still living at home, and even those who are refugees, those teens express hope for the future.

Ibrahim was thirteen years old when ISIS occupied his hometown of Deir el-Zour. The soldiers started to slowly indoctrinate him. He became a soldier for them. Though his mother helped free him from ISIS—not once but twice—Ibrahim had a hard time breaking the terrorists' spell over him. Plus, he told *PBS NewsHour* in 2016, he did not know how he could simply return home. He had witnessed and participated in too many horrific acts. What he and all the other young people in Syria witnessed "will make this generation a cruel generation," he said.

Protecting Loved Ones

UPI painted a stirring image of a teen soldier in a 2016 article on child soldiers in Syria. Months before, maybe even years before, a wealthy family had fled the fighting. They abandoned their mansion. Abu al-Baraa was one of their countrymen who stayed in Syria. He was not a member of the elite. He had dropped out of school at age thirteen. But at age fifteen, he would find himself living in the mansion. He spent his days there, sitting in a gold chair, holding a sniper rifle. "I sit here to protect myself and my family," he told UPI. He sought out a rebel group because he wanted

DANGEROUS LOVE

Some teenagers join ISIS not because they believe the terrorist group's ideology. Rather, they follow the person they're dating into ISIS. Some even turn to ISIS to find love. In 2014, Marlin Stivani Nivarlain was a fourteen-year-old living in Sweden. She dropped out of school. She got a new boyfriend, and he showed her the ISIS propaganda videos he'd been watching.

"And I don't know anything about Islam or ISIS or something, so I didn't know what he meant. Then he said he want[ed] to go to ISIS, and I said OK, no problem," she later told a Middle East news station.

By May of 2015, Marlin and her boyfriend had traveled to Syria. ISIS members met them there. They then took them to a house in Iraq. Immediately, Marlin realized her mistake. Life was nothing like it had been for her in Sweden. "It was really a hard life," she said. The ISIS house she lived in didn't even have running water. Fortunately, she found a way to call her mother. Her mom contacted Swedish authorities. In early 2016, they asked Kurdish special forces to rescue Marlin.

ISIS itself sees romantic relationships as a recruitment strategy. The terrorist group even uses "online dating" types of websites to recruit women to join ISIS. ISIS prints gushing passages that read like romance novels or diary entries. These

Vandals defaced this image of President Assad in Aleppo. But young people do more than commit acts of vandalism, and a romantic relationship can be a recruitment strategy.

make ISIS seem like a matchmaking service. Women can become brides for its soldiers.

Dr. Mia Bloom, author of *Dying to Kill*, told CNN that for these women "it's about making everything bad in their life go away because now they're going to have the perfect future." ISIS promises the women free housing, health care, and cars. In exchange, they marry ISIS fighters.

In reality, the women are themselves trained to fight. They aren't allowed to choose whom they marry. They live in squalid conditions. When a husband is killed, his widow is forced to marry another waiting soldier.

to fight. "Everyone else fled to Europe and Turkey, and they left us here without protection."

Acting Out Aggression

Andre Poulin was a young Canadian who spent his teen years and his early twenties learning how to build explosives from the internet. He was arrested multiple times for making violent threats against the people he was sharing a house with. The prosecutor in his cases told the *New York Times* in 2014 that Poulin had admitted to his actions. "He said he doesn't care if he went to jail. Then he says nobody is going to help him and that everybody is out to get him. He said something had to be done, and he talked about sacrificing himself."

Poulin, who changed his name to Abu Muslim, converted to Islam. The last time anyone heard from him in Canada was after he served two weeks in jail in 2010. He was probably around twenty-one years old at that time. The next time he appeared was in an ISIS recruitment video. He spoke about leading a normal, well-adjusted life in Canada. ISIS's mission spoke to him, he said. He believed it was honorable to fight. In the video, he urged others to send money, lend their skills, or join him in battle too. The final scenes show him running through a field in Syria. He and his fellow ISIS soldiers were attacking an airport. He died in that battle.

A Confluence of Reasons to Join

Teenagers fight in Syria for many reasons. They may feel desperate and like they have no other option in life. They may feel lonely and isolated. To some teens, joining a terrorist organization or a military can seem like they are finding community and making friends. They may also be angry and seeking revenge or justice. After years of fighting, the Syrian Civil War has claimed many lives. Many teens have watched family and friends die, and they may want to fight against the groups that killed their loved ones.

Teens may do horrible things while they are soldiers or acting with terrorist organizations. However, as young people, they are also victims. They are vulnerable to being forced to fight. They are sometimes kidnapped by terrorist groups. Teens are also are deeply affected by war even if they are not active participants in the fighting. Their schools are bombed and destroyed. They live in fear in cities that have been taken over by terrorists or are forced to flee their homes and become refugees in another country. Teens are recruited into terrorism and fighting, but they also suffer some of the biggest losses of war.

The city and people of Kobani have suffered enormously during the Syrian Civil War.

CHAPTER FOUR

THE YOUNGEST CASUALTIES OF THE SYRIAN CIVIL WAR

There were many reasons the Syrian Civil War *could* happen. A long history of social, political, and environmental events made the conditions just right in 2011 for a major and complicated conflict to take root and spread. However, there was only one event that ignited the situation so that the civil war *did* happen—and that event revolved around the actions of a group of teenagers.

It may seem strange to tell the story of what started the Syrian Civil War so late in this book. It's not. If these teenagers had not acted and been caught, another event would have started the war. There was no way to stop the Arab Spring from reaching Syria. Therefore, the teenagers' story is less about their role beginning the war and more about how they became the first "casualties" of the war.

"Your Turn, Doctor"

February 16, 2011, was a cold, still winter night. Naief Abazid stood giggling with his friends outside their all-boys school in the town of Daraa in southern Syria. At fourteen, he was the youngest. They egged him on to spray-paint a message in red under the principal's office window: "Your turn, Doctor." Then, that was it. The prank was over. They all went home. "It was something silly," Naief told the *Globe and Mail* five years later. "I was a kid. I didn't know what I was doing … I only realized it was serious when I got to prison."

The "doctor" was Syrian President Assad. He was an ophthalmologist, an eye doctor, before his father died and he took over the presidency. What the teens meant by "your turn" was that Syria was next in line to experience an Arab Spring. Just as massive public protests had forced Tunisian and Egyptian leaders out of office, the boys were saying that Syrians would take down the Syrian government.

Arrest, Detention, and Torture

Naief was called to the principal's office when he returned to school. He was told he was meeting with someone from the Education Ministry about the graffiti. They knew he was involved because this was not his first time spray-painting the school. They knew his handwriting.

The man was actually from Syria's internal security force, the mukhabarat. As soon as they got outside, Naief was pushed into a waiting car and handcuffed. As they drove away, the men in the car punched him. At the mukhabarat office, the torture continued.

For the next ten days, Naief lived in a tiny prison cell. Every hour or so, the guards would beat him. Eventually, he gave the men the names of five other teenagers who had been at the school the night of the vandalism. Those five were arrested and tortured until they gave up more names—and so on, until the government had arrested twenty-three teenagers.

Omar was a classmate who had not been with the group that night and was not named. He was friends with some of the boys, however. He told *Vice* in 2016 that he spent the weeks his friends were imprisoned keeping their families company. "How can you sleep at night, when you know your friends are being tortured?" he asked. Even those who were left free were being tortured, with worry and fear.

The parents of the boys finally secured a meeting with Atef Najib, head of security in the town. He was also President Assad's cousin. According to a *Globe and Mail* source, Najib told the parents, "'Forget about your children. Go have new kids.'" It sounded like the boys would never be set free. Of course, their parents refused to give up hope.

On March 18, a month after the boys had been arrested, the people protested in the streets of Daraa. It would come to be known as the Day of Rage. Not long into the protest, police snipers started shooting. Two protesters were killed. A few days later, the police opened fire on mourners attending the funerals. Several were killed.

A Moment of Celebration

Assad then released the twenty-three bruised and battered teenagers. His plan to calm the city worked, for a very short time. The citizens were understandably so thrilled to have the boys back that they started celebrating. "It was like a wedding," Naief told the *Globe and Mail*. "I didn't understand why they were calling us heroes. I just wanted to go home and see my mother."

Naief soon understood why they considered him a hero. They saw him as standing up to the administration—and surviving. Now other people were no longer afraid to demand reform from the president. This was similar to what had happened in Tunisia just a couple months earlier. One person's actions, though tragic, inspired other people to act. After the celebration on the day of the boys' release, protesters took to the streets again.

A Tragic Symbol of the Revolution

Those protests were the beginning of rebellion. Hardly a day went by without a demonstration happening. Teenagers had been some of the first to protest. They had done so in support of their imprisoned classmates. After their friends' release, they continued to join in the demonstrations.

Hamza Ali al-Khateeb was one of those teens. He was arrested April 29, 2011, at a protest in the town of Jiza, near Daraa. The Daraa boys were held without word for a month, and no one knew Hamza's fate for a month either. Tragically, that was where the similarities end. Hamza's body, covered in gruesome marks of torture, was returned to his family. The entire country felt grief and anger. "Hamza has become a symbol of the Syrian revolution," Radwan Ziadeh, an exiled Syrian human rights activist, told the *New York Times*.

A School Trip That Ended in Terror

Education is very important to many Syrians. Even during wartime, they still leave their homes to attend classes. So, with an eye toward the future, 186 boys aged fourteen to sixteen boarded ten minibuses for a school-sponsored trip on May 30, 2014. They boys lived in the Kobani province on Syria's border with Turkey. They needed to get to the city of Aleppo to take a test. Syria requires all students to pass this exam.

Their parents, along with the parents of other teens from Kobani, prepared their children well for the journey. For example, the girls wore the full niqab. All of the children were instructed not to bring anything with them that might tell an ISIS soldier where they were from. The students also traveled together in the buses so they would not be driving alone. Kobani has been a hotspot in the Syrian Civil War. Most of the people who live there are Kurdish, an ethnic group that has strongly resisted ISIS. The parents wanted their children to blend in and not make any ISIS soldiers along the route suspicious that they were from the resistance. Nothing happened on the way to the exam.

In October 2014, an explosion could be seen in Kobani, likely from a US-led coalition airstrike.

On the boys' way home, however, their lives changed. A troop of ISIS soldiers stopped the boys' buses. They forced the drivers to reroute the convoy to a religious school in the town of Minbej. They said they were going to give the boys "reform" lessons in the Quran and in jihad.

Mustafa Hassan was one of the students. He told the *Guardian* later that the ISIS fighters were clearly from all over the world. "I saw a lot of Russians, Chechens. Libyans, some Saudi Arabians and Syrians too."

Mere hours into his imprisonment at the school, Mustafa was planning his escape. The days passed. He grew even more desperate to get out, even though the ISIS fighters threatened them with death if they tried to escape. Life was too scary at the school to stay.

"If the students were loud or chaotic, they were beaten with an electrical cable," Mustafa told the *Guardian*. "Ten boys were beaten every day. But most of us were well-behaved, to not get beaten. Some of the boys were crying, some turned yellow with fear. They showed us a documentary film from Iraq: of people being slaughtered."

After four days in captivity, Mustafa saw his chance to escape. Classmates began peppering their ISIS teacher with questions. In the confusion, Mustafa and another boy said they would go to the roof to fetch some water and raise the flag. The teacher let them go as the questions from the others continued.

The two boys jumped from the roof to a lower part of the school and then to the ground. They hurried into the nearby town of Menbej. Civilians there helped them to return home. A month after the abduction, most of the boys were still being held. Their parents were also like hostages. They were consumed by rumors about their children. They were told they had been killed. Then they were told they had been released. They were told the boys were part of a prisoner exchange deal being worked out. Then they were told to go to a checkpoint because their children were returning, but they were not. One official said ISIS demanded the parents protest their local leaders.

"I am in a bad situation, psychologically so bad and confused," one father told the *Guardian*. Some parents called friends in Menbej, but those people told them they had nothing to do with the kidnapping. They could not help. Kobani became a "haunted, desperate city," the *Guardian* wrote. Fifteen of the 186 teenagers were eventually released as part of a prisoner exchange. Besides them, Mustafa, and the friend who escaped with him, everyone else is still at the Menbej school. "Everyone knows a parent with a missing child."

Two Hostage Stories from the ISIS Capital City

In October 2017, Syrian and American forces were days away from liberating the Syrian town of Raqqa. This was important because ISIS considered Raqqa its capital city. If anti-ISIS troops could push the terrorist group out the city, that would weaken ISIS considerably. More than that, it would be, in essence, a huge hostage rescue.

ISIS had held the city as its own for three years. Most of Raqqa's citizens had fled before ISIS arrived. However, around two thousand civilians had not escaped. Once ISIS took over, they could no longer escape. CBS News reported that they were "trapped and … unable to escape the small area controlled by ISIS gunmen." The 250 ISIS fighters occupied the hospital and other buildings. They used the civilians as human shields.

One man, a taxi driver who did manage to escape Raqqa, told CBS News a horrifying example of why most citizens did not even dare try to escape. One time, ISIS dragged a woman into the middle of the city. They gathered everyone else around and auctioned her off as a slave. "They'd shout '100 dollars for this one,'" the man said. "They did it to terrify us, to show they could do it to us if we didn't obey them."

As anti-ISIS Syrian and US troops approached Raqqa in October 2017, a CBS News correspondent traveling with them interviewed a group of women who had just escaped the city. One said something surprising: "I'm from Kansas."

She was just fifteen years old. She was also six months pregnant. She had been forced to marry a Syrian ISIS fighter. He had recently been killed. The teenager's father had brought her to Syria against her will five years earlier, when she was ten. She was a devout Muslim, but she hated ISIS. Her father, however, was an ISIS supporter. When he was killed, she was a young girl completely alone in an unfamiliar and dangerous land.

"We were prisoners. We were just quiet. Shut up, sit down you're in the house, you have nothing to say," she told the reporter. She said that every moment they were happy they hadn't yet been killed. She had seen so much violence in her five years with ISIS. Walking along the streets in the city was like walking through a horror movie.

"Hi, Mom," she said into the reporter's camera. "If you see this video, please contact me." She said, "I still have hope, hope to go to school, hope to be a normal person, hope to be a mother to my child."

As Quick as a Cup of Coffee

Mohammed Qatta was a fourteen-year-old coffee vendor in Aleppo, Syria. One day he quipped to a customer, "Even if [Prophet] Mohammed comes back to life, I won't." The boy and the prophet shared the same name, though the boy usually went by his nickname, Salmo.

Supporters of al-Qaeda happened to be driving by at that moment. They overheard him. They considered what

Residents drink coffee and walk through Aleppo a month after the government military reclaimed the city from the rebel forces.

he said blasphemy, making fun of Islam's prophet. They grabbed Salmo and dragged him away.

They returned to the square later. Salmo was with them. He clearly had been beaten. They announced that they were charging him with the crime of blasphemy. The terrorists then killed him in front of his family and the public.

Refugees

Syrian refugees are being held hostage by the actions of their government. Because they are looking for a new home country, they are also at the mercy of the governments of other countries, such as the United States.

As of 2017, more than 6.5 million people were displaced within Syria. They had to flee their homes, but they have not left their country. Another 4.9 million are refugees. They have left Syria. Half of these are children. Three-quarters of the Syrian refugees who arrived in the United States between fall 2015 and 2016 were women and children.

We met Fatmeh earlier in this book. Her family had the beautiful house with the lovely garden in Syria. She had loved Arabic literature. Since becoming a refugee in Lebanon, her life has not been her own. Her family had to repay the debt they owed the Lebanese farmer who helped them settle in to their new home. At fifteen years old, Fatmeh worked up to fourteen hours a day in the farmer's fields.

She picked onions, cucumbers, and potatoes. He paid her about eight US dollars a day. He did not give her that money but instead subtracted it from what her family owed

A refugee from Aleppo does laundry at an unofficial refugee camp in Lebanon in 2015.

him. When his foreman thought any of the kids weren't working hard enough, he whacked them with a plastic pipe.

Hussin was twelve years old when soldiers burst into her family's home in Daraa, Syria. The soldiers destroyed or stole everything in the house. Then they threatened to kill Hussin. Somehow, her mother convinced them not to. The soldiers left. That did not mean that Hussin and her family were "free" again, as they had been. All their possessions were either broken or gone. Of more concern, they feared for their lives. They were hostages to the soldiers' whims. The family left immediately. Eventually, they became refugees in Jordan.

In 2015, then-President Obama said the United States would start taking more Syrian refugees than it ever had before. The governors of thirty states called on Obama to cancel or at least pause his plan. Most said their reason was security concerns. Many courts and citizens alike disagreed with their local leaders. They wanted to welcome refugees from Syria and offer them support.

In 2017, President Trump issued an executive order banning Syrian refugees from entering the United States. Again, the courts and the people protested. As *Teen Vogue* reported, there have been no fatal terrorist attacks in the United States by refugees: "The odds of being killed by a refugee terrorist are 3.6 billion to 1." Larry Bartlett, director of the office of Refugee Admissions at the State Department,

"LIKE A WINTER FOG"

People search for survivors of an attack on the town of Khan Shaykhun, Syria, in October 2017.

Early on April 4, 2017, warplanes attacked the Syrian town of Khan Sheikhoun. Fourteen-year-old Mariam Abu Khalil was awake and looking out her window at just that moment. She became a witness interviewed by the media.

She reported seeing an aircraft drop a bomb on a one-story building. A yellow mushroom cloud "like a winter fog" rose up from the building. As it would turn out, Mariam was lucky she was at home, where she didn't have to breathe the poisoned air. First responders to the site of the explosion found people, including children, collapsed on the street. They were choking and in pain.

US intelligence agencies reported that the Syrian government attacked its people with sarin gas. They did so in retaliation for a rebel attack against the government. Sarin is considered twenty times as deadly as cyanide. It is colorless, odorless, and tasteless, so it gives its victims no warning. Sarin causes the heart and muscles involved in breathing to spasm. Death can occur within minutes of exposure.

One day after the attack, Canadian Prime Minister Justin Trudeau said he and his country were "shocked and appalled" at the attack. Believing it was "critical" that Canada respond immediately, he pledged 840 million Canadian dollars in life-saving humanitarian and development efforts for Syrian citizens.

told the magazine that "refugees undergo a rigorous application process that lasts between eighteen and twenty-four months on average, and involves being vetted by the National Counterterrorism Center, the FBI, the Department of Homeland Security, the Department of Defense, as well as other agencies. They also undergo medical screening." Once refugees are in the United States, they start leading their own independent lives. Ruben Chandrasekar, an executive director of the International Rescue Committee, says, "Within four to six months, 85 percent start working, paying their bills, paying taxes, and becoming self-sufficient."

Free Hostages

Syria can be a terrifying place. Fighting from multiple sides is constantly happening, even in civilian areas. Teenagers can feel like hostages to the violence even if they're technically free and living at home.

In August 2015, Mercy Corps released the results of a survey. They had talked with 120 Syrian teens, two hundred parents, and local community figures around the country. According to the *Economist*'s analysis of the report, all Syrian teens felt unsafe in the present and uncertain about their future.

While 81 percent said they were still attending school, 76 percent felt their education was being threatened. Many Syrians rank a good education over good health, so they will risk a lot to keep going to school. However, the teens' survey answers indicated they were also aware of the bleak reality. In 2015, a quarter of the country's schools had been destroyed. Even if they still had a school to attend today, it might be bombed tomorrow.

Around 80 percent of Syrian teens did not go out after dark. Of those who did, most were boys. They went out at night usually without their parents' permission. "Given the dangers," according to an article in the *Economist*, their anxious parents see "this … as a death-wish rather than a normal act of adolescent rebellion." About 74 percent of teens went straight to school and straight home after. And 61 percent would have liked to participate in extracurricular activities but feared for their safety. If they could go out to participate in an activity, they said, it would be learning first aid. They knew that medical help was scarce. Eight in ten responding to Mercy Corps' survey said they didn't have access to a hospital because theirs had been destroyed.

Because they were aware of how much terrorist organizations use social media to recruit young people, most teens had stopped discussing anything remotely political online. They did not want to attract the attention of terrorists.

Kobani, the province where the 186 abducted high-schoolers were from, offered examples of this kind of "free hostage" situation. According to an August 2014 *Newsweek* article, Kobani residents had not had any electricity for six months. ISIS controlled the water supply that generated the electricity. ISIS cut off that connection "to choke Kobani into submission."

Kobani residents said they lived in a "through-the-keyhole world." This meant they did not have freedom of movement. They were constantly peering quietly out of their houses, checking that it was safe. They moved about "at their peril" and faced "the ever-present risk that their whole way of life might suddenly collapse," said the article in *Newsweek*. The people were "stranded here indefinitely."

Rozana was an eighteen-year-old girl who spoke to *Newsweek* about her plans to leave rural Kobani for the city of Aleppo to study and then work. Her parents forbid her from leaving. Their decision may have saved her life, but she was then "trapped in suffocating limbo." She could not take her college entrance exams or hope to attend school for at least another year. She also did not know what to do in Kobani. "It's safe here," she said. "But it's a big prison."

Different Definitions of Resilience

War has changed Syrian teens' lives. All of them are affected by it daily. This has required them to make changes, big and small, in their lives. They have to adjust how, when, and where they travel, where they live, and what their hopes are for the future. They have also had to call on and develop their resilience. Syrian teens, it turns out, have an interesting way of being resilient.

In the summer of 2017, NPR reported on a new study about resiliency. Specifically, researchers interviewed Syrian tweens and teens who had been displaced because of their country's civil war. They wanted to know how these young people had "the strength to endure" such extreme hardship.

"In the West, we tend to think of resilience as inner psychological strength," Catherine Panter-Brick, an anthropologist who worked on the study, told NPR. "In the Middle East, resilience is more of a collective and social strength."

NPR interviewed some of the teenagers from the study. A fifteen-year-old girl said resilience was "to mix with people, to not be introverted or alone." A sixteen-year-old boy said resilience meant "that I have Jordanian friends." All of the teens said they drew strength from integrating into their new communities, going to school, making new friends, and continuing to work toward their dreams. Resilience, for them, was not about being tough.

The researchers saw benefit in these answers because they were so positive. They would help keep the teens' spirits up. "When you start asking them about resilience, it helps them to look at their cup as half full rather than half empty," Rana Dajani, a biologist who helped with the work, told NPR. The researchers used their findings to develop a survey. Humanitarian aid groups could use it to track whether their programs were helping young refugees.

Building Empathy

Lina Sergie Attar is a Syrian American who founded the Karam Foundation, which supports Syrians in rebuilding their lives. She also writes articles about her experiences and opinions of the Syrian Civil War.

In an editorial for the *New York Times* in 2016, she wrote that "a favorite tool of the dispassionate Syria analyst is a map: red and green blobs showing a shifting front line, which streets are held by rebels and which by the government. These wretched maps rudely superimpose their lines over the landmarks of my life."

What she was saying was that the media can too easily turn real people and places into cold facts and figures. Data is important to collect and understand, but not at the expense of dehumanizing individuals. People in war zones may be alive and free from imprisonment or abduction, but if the world sees them only as a collection of numbers in a table or dots and lines on a graph, those people are, in essence, hostages of their situation.

In 2013, Attar countered this kind of mapping with her own. She traveled to Atmeh, the largest refugee camp on the Syrian border. There, she led a group of children in "mapping memory." She explained the activity to the children as she drew:

> *"This is where I used to sit for lunch every day with my mother and my father and my brother and my other brother." I drew the round table and colored it blue. I drew our living room, my bedroom and the large balcony where I spent so many June days just like that one. "This is where I used to read, this is where I used to watch TV, this is where I used to …"*

For every fact we read about Syria, we would do well to link it in our minds to something like a blue-colored kitchen table. There are real people behind Syria's war.

POPULATION: REFUGEE

Erie, Pennsylvania, is a small town. It had fewer than one hundred thousand people in 2016. Its diversity, however, is vast. Around 10 percent of Erie residents moved there as refugees. They came from Poland, Italy, Germany, Ireland, and Russia in the twentieth century. In the twenty-first century, they came from Somalia, Congo, Bhutan, Iraq, and Syria.

In 2016, President Obama increased the number of Syrian refugees the United States would accept that year to ten thousand. The Syrian population around Erie swelled. Ninety-one Syrians were relocated to the area in July 2016 alone. By August 2016, at least three hundred lived in Erie.

At the same time, then-presidential candidate Donald Trump held a rally in Erie and expressed concern about the influx of Syrian refugees. According to an *Atlantic* magazine article written about the town's refugees, the residents disagreed. "The more immigrants or refugees settled in the communities, the less concern there was about the upsets or risks they might bring," the article explained.

Mohammad and Yasmine Zkrit, along with their two young daughters, escaped their home city of Aleppo after their neighborhood was bombed by government forces. They spent three years as refugees in Jordan. During that time, they had two more children. Finally, they were offered the chance to resettle in Erie. They now have a new home.

Raqqa was finally freed from ISIS militants on October 20, 2017, but the damage to the city is severe.

CHAPTER FIVE

SOLVING TERROR IN SYRIA

In a war like Syria's, it can be easy to feel doubtful that the violence will ever end. There are so many powerful groups fighting. It seems like they will never stop. There has been so much destruction already. It seems too hard to pull out of that. The days feel likely to continue to spiral into more ruin. Yet early in November 2017, the Syrian military forced ISIS out of the last city it controlled, Boukamal, near Syria's border with Iraq. ABC News reported that General Ali Mayhoub called this win "a declaration of the fall of [ISIS's] project in the region generally and the collapse of its supporters' illusions to divide it, control large parts of the Syria-Iraq borders and secure supply routes between the two countries." ISIS still very much exists, but its members in Syria are believed to be scattered in the desert and small towns. Military experts hope this means those terrorists cannot communicate easily with each other and mobilize into a stronger force.

Of course, even major successes do not mean the situation in Syria is stable and its people are safe. For example, the US military knew that driving ISIS from Raqqa in October 2017 would not be the final step to total peace. Lieutenant General Steve Townsend, in charge of the coalition battling ISIS in Syria, spoke with CBS News about this in 2017. He said that American troops probably would be in the country "a while" longer. Even if ISIS lost all of its Syrian territory, it would not disappear. It would become an insurgency in the rural areas of Syria. "That's the next stage of ISIS," Townsend said. "We call that ISIS 2.0."

As soldiers continue to try to make progress within the very big challenge that is the Syrian War, civilians are making bold moves too.

Syrian Youth Taking Action

Every day Syrians survive can be considered a major victory. However, survival is not always enough. Humans are built to hope, plan for the future, and thrive. Even while trying to survive day to day, Syrians are making the strange and often horrible world they live in better, for themselves and for

BOMBS AGAINST BOMBS

Taylor Wilson invents devices to detect terrorist weapons.

In 2009, Taylor Wilson was a regular fifteen-year-old kid, except that he liked to build bombs. His passion started just because he was interested in the science. He had no idea he'd ultimately use his skills to fight terrorism.

At ten years old, Wilson built his first bomb out of a pill bottle and chemicals he found around his home. At eleven, he was buying vials of plutonium online. At fourteen, he became the youngest person ever to build a nuclear fusion reactor. Needless to say, he caught the attention of the US government. The US Department of Homeland Security invited him to their offices. They were impressed by their conversation with him. They suggested he apply for a research grant.

In an interview with CNN in 2011, when he was seventeen, Taylor said, "I wanted a real challenge. So I decided to try fighting terrorists." He began developing devices that can detect radiation in high-risk countries.

Taylor is a big fan of other teens stepping up and effecting change too. He told CNN that he considered his age not a problem but an asset. "Kids haven't been exposed to the bureaucracy of professional science, they're a lot more open to trying things," he explained. "In that way, I think kids are able to sometimes do better science than adults."

others. Sometimes this is done in small ways, like checking in on neighbors. Sometimes individuals take bigger steps.

Leadership During Wartime

Lina Sergie Attar, the founder of the Karam Foundation, does more than help people empathize with Syrians. Her foundation donates money to projects that help people. Attar was born in the United States but spent her teen years in Aleppo, Syria. She even earned one of her college degrees there. When the civil war in Syria broke out, she refocused her foundation on Syria. Attar wanted to help her fellow Syrians rebuild.

A large part of Karam's work is in education. School is increasingly unavailable for young people, particularly girls. School buildings are being destroyed in the war. Families are having to flee their homes for refugee camps. Girls are quitting school to help care for their families during this ongoing emergency.

One of Karam's educational programs is the Karam Leadership Program (KLP). It trains displaced teenagers in how to rebuild their futures. Three hundred Syrian high school students attended KLP's first series of workshops, in November 2014. Professionals from different businesses taught them about team-building; developing a life plan; technology; and journalism and media. The students learned about product development and e-commerce as well as basic business and entrepreneurial skills. They also talked about learning the Turkish and English languages and how to prepare for tests to get into college.

Syrian Snow Whites

Rua Ismael was an eleven-year-old girl living in Salamiyeh, Syria. And then, in an instant, she was gone. On January 25, 2013, she was killed during a terrorist bombing. People were devastated that such a young person was killed. They gave her a loving nickname, Syria's Snow White.

Four years later, girls about the age Rua was found their own link to Snow White. The *Hindu* newspaper reported their story. The article does not report that there was an intentional connection between Rua and these girls. However, it's a nice idea that Rua's legacy lives on through other young people in Syria. In a country where the youngest of children are aware they may die, it is heartening when they can reclaim their childhood stories.

That's exactly what thirteen girls in the town of Douma, outside of Damascus, did. They learned and performed *Snow White and the Seven Dwarfs* in a sold-out theater. By doing this, they were practicing self-care. There are so many young people in Syria who know, or remember, only war. International aid group Save the Children has said that their

Thirteen Syrian girls perform *Snow White and the Seven Dwarfs.*

whole generation may be "lost to trauma and extreme stress." Children are fighting against terrorism when they find joy in their lives.

"It was really hard, but I memorized all my lines in English," ten-year-old Afnan, who played the Queen, told the *Hindu.* "When I act, I forget the war that we're living through in Douma, and I feel happy and hopeful."

It says a lot that theater could help her that much. Her region had been under regular attack by the government because there were rebels there. It was not unusual, the *Hindu* reported, for children in Afnan's town to be injured or killed even while they were walking to school. Days before the final performance of *Snow White*, the director's husband was killed by a stray bullet.

Still, Rayhana, the eleven-year-old who played Snow White, could only see the good. She said her favorite part of the play was her character "escaping a tragic fate." Rayhana, Afnan, and their friends learned to keep that kind of hope alive in real life too.

You Can Do Something

Syria may feel far away, but anyone can help in the fight against terror. Terrorist organizations prey on people who are feeling lonely and like they do not belong anywhere. If there's not a sense of community somewhere, people are more likely to be influenced by anyone who offers to include them in a group. This happens to adults, teens, and kids. So, one of the main ways you can keep your part of the world safe is to stay connected with the people who are physically closest to you: your family, your friends, your neighbors, and your classmates and teachers. Furthermore, if disaster strikes—a war or natural devastation like hurricane or fire—chaos will be less likely to follow. People will be prepared, remain calmer, and help each other.

The New York State Police have offered suggestions on how teens can help in the fight against terrorism and ensure their communities are prepared for emergencies. The following are some of their ideas:

- Sign up with the Red Cross, the Salvation Army, or another emergency-response organization as a volunteer.

- Speak up at public hearings for the needs and concerns of youth and children in emergency situations. Work with other young people to come up with a list of ways you can help and ways the community can help you.

- Sign up (if you are old enough, which depends on your area) as a volunteer firefighter, or attend a citizens' or a youth academy, if your police department offers one.

Donate as a Group

Of course, it is also important to help those currently in need. With homes, schools, and livelihoods destroyed, and futures feeling terribly uncertain, Syrians need a hand staying fed, clothed, and sheltered now and rebuilding later.

Foundations and individuals in need often need cash most of all. Always talk with an adult you trust before sending your money to someone. Then make your donating fun—and

A Syrian youth carries an aid package from the Syrian Red Crescent.

make an even bigger impact—by inviting friends, classmates, family, and neighbors to donate with you.

The Karam Foundation offers a neat way to do this. On its website, it lists different "items" and the costs to achieve them. For example, you could donate to Karam House, "a community-led center of leadership for Syrian refugee teens where they can learn STEAM-focused skills." The donation requested for that is $250. Or you could mobilize your community to make a $10,000 donation to help rebuild a school in Syria. From relatively little to relatively big, a person's gift of any amount can make a huge impact.

Karam's approach is fun and interesting because you know exactly where your money will go. If helping a family receive winter coats and hats sounds appealing to you, you can fund-raise for that. If supporting education scholarships for high school and college students is important, you can choose that.

Karam does not expect you to give all that money from your own wallet. Its website allows you to donate by yourself or as part of a team. You can join a team already in existence or create your own. You could consider talking with your family, friends, school, neighborhood, or religious or activity group to form a team. Each person on your team could then ask the people they knew to contribute. Even if just a couple of your friends come together with you, with each of your networks, you will find you'll be able to raise more funds.

The National Syrian Project for Prosthetic Limbs offers a similar idea on its website. This project is operated by UK-based Syria Relief. It builds prosthetics: artificial arms and legs. It also offers physical therapy. For as many people that have been killed in the Syrian Civil War, there are many more who have been injured. A war zone is never easy to navigate. If a person has an injured or amputated arm or leg, getting around is even more difficult. Physical therapy is also not common in Syria, so people have a harder time retraining their bodies to work well after an injury.

Despite the great need for help for those with injured limbs, few organizations put their donation budgets toward rehabilitation. So, the National Syrian Project for Prosthetic Limbs is a good, and often overlooked, place to donate to. It lists several donation ideas you may want to participate in or replicate. One of their donors raised money by drawing nonstop for twenty-four hours. People pledged money in support of her reaching that goal, and the money went to the project. Another person teamed up with his teenage sons. They pledged to climb the highest mountains in Scotland, England, and Wales in one weekend. They asked their friends to give money in support of this, which they then passed on to the project. You can donate in support of these ideas, or you (and your friends) can create your own idea and ask people to support your efforts.

Support Syrian Refugees

Teen Vogue has offered great ideas for helping Syrian refugees, including becoming a family mentor. There are international, national, and local organizations that work with refugees and look for volunteers. Find one and ask how you can be paired with a Syrian family new to your town. You may help provide them with supplies—most refugees arrive in their new homes with very little. You may also help them learn how to get around their new city or help them practice English. At the most basic level, you can be a friendly face in a town of strangers, someone they can turn to when they feel lonely or uncertain—and, really, there is nothing basic about that.

Creating welcome kits is another way to help. Refugees have to leave most things behind when they flee their homes. Sometimes, the things they do bring with them get stolen before they reach their new home in your city. Sometimes they have to trade items to pay for travel, food, or shelter before a country accepts them into a permanent home. So when a family arrives in your town, they likely will not have even basic bathroom and kitchen supplies. Create care packages for them. Include fun things—these are also important!—like clothing and toys and books. The organization that is helping the refugees travel to your town can tell you what items will be most needed.

Finally, *Teen Vogue* suggests calling your elected representatives. Even if you are too young to vote, you are still a constituent, a person your elected officials are supposed to serve. They want to hear from you. Ask them never to pass laws against refugees and to support accepting as many newcomers fleeing war as possible. As the magazine says, "Those fleeing persecution deserve compassion and can make positive contributions to society."

More Work to Be Done

The Syrian Civil War demonstrates just how complicated terrorism is: power vacuums, geographic characteristics, economic circumstances, and more combine to form some of today's worst terrorist organizations. The situation in Syria also demonstrates how unstoppable war can feel.

In February 2018, nearly seven years after the Syrian Civil War started, the fighting increased. The *Washington Post* said the war was "rapidly descending into a global scramble for control over what remains of the broken country of Syria." Sami Nadir, of the Levant Institute for Strategic Affairs, told the newspaper that "the risks are high" and "any escalation could pave the way for a regional or international war." More and more powerful countries—from the United States to Russia to Israel, Iran, Iraq, and Lebanon—are involved in increasingly direct ways. The complexity is not lessening, the violence is growing, and the need for help is big. Young people around the world can stay aware of what is happening in Syria and how their countries are involved. Syrian teens, both those still in the country and those displaced and living as refugees, need to be remembered and supported. They are fighting for their future, which is tied up with the future of us all.

A WORLD OF DIFFERENCE ON A SPREADSHEET

You don't have to start or even join an organization to make a difference in the world. In 2016, nineteen-year-old Heraa Hashmi changed minds for the better with a humble spreadsheet.

Heraa was studying molecular biology at the University of Colorado Boulder. A fellow student challenged her with a brazen claim. He said that Muslims never denounce acts of terrorism by Islamic terrorists. As a Muslim American, Heraa thought she might know better than her classmate. She also knew she would not change his mind unless she presented him with clear facts.

For about two hours every day for the next three weeks, she built a shareable and editable Google spreadsheet. On this spreadsheet, she recorded the times Muslim groups and leaders condemned terrorism. Finally, she decided to pause and see how many cases she had listed. There were 5,720 instances of Muslims saying they disagreed with terrorism.

Heraa thought, why share this only with that one classmate? She had put a lot of work into it. She also had a lot of Twitter followers. She could share this information with so many people. She explained in an interview, "Things like this often go unnoticed outside the Muslim community, and I wanted to bring them to light." Perhaps at least in part because of people like Heraa speaking out, more news stories are talking about this. For example, CBS News wrote in 2017 that ISIS does not equate with the faith of Islam. It proclaims "a twisted version of Islam that is unrecognizable to most Muslims."

So, Heraa prepared an answer for her classmate—and answered in a very big way. On Saturday, November 12, 2016, she tweeted a link to her spreadsheet. By the time *Teen Vogue* interviewed her on Monday, November 14, the tweet had been shared twelve thousand times. Two other people had turned the list into an interactive website.

Heraa told *Teen Vogue* she wished she didn't have to defend her religion. She also didn't want to need to educate others. She wanted them to care enough to educate themselves. Even when she was a kid, strangers would ask her questions about her background. "I hated how I had to respond for my entire country and my entire religion," she told *Teen Vogue*. "And in many ways it's still the same, but I started to realize that each difference is actually a connection to more people, more ideas, and more experiences."

CHRONOLOGY

700,000 years ago
People begin to live where modern-day Syria now is.

1516   The Ottoman Empire conquers Syria.

1840   The first major European involvement in Syria begins.

1920   Syria becomes a French colony.

1946   Syria gains independence.

2000   Bashar al-Assad becomes president of Syria.

2001–2011
Dust storms and severe drought cause major problems in Syria.

2011   The Arab Spring starts in Tunisia and Egypt.

2011   The Syrian Civil War starts.

2017   Half of Syria's prewar population is dead, injured, internally displaced from their homes, or living as refugees in countries other than Syria.

GLOSSARY

al-Qaeda A militant Islamist organization founded by Osama bin Laden in the 1980s.

Arab Spring A period of pro-democracy protests in the Middle East that began in 2010.

coup A sudden, violent, and illegal seizure of power from a government.

Daesh A name for ISIS that is not recognized by ISIS supporters.

dissident A person who opposes official government policy.

groom To prepare a person for a particular purpose.

infidel A person who follows no religion or a religion different from the person who calls them that.

insurgency A condition of revolt against a government that is less than an organized revolution and that is not recognized as belligerency.

ISIS Islamic State of Iraq and Syria, an extremist organization known for its gruesome violence. The terrorist group is also known as the Islamic State (IS) and the Islamic State of Iraq and the Levant (ISIL).

jihad A struggle against the enemies of Islam.

militant A person who is aggressive in support of a political or social cause.

mukhabarat The Arabic term for "intelligence," as in "intelligence agency." Syria's intelligence agency is known by this term.

radicalized A person who has adopted extreme political or social positions.

refugee A person who has been forced to leave their country because of war, persecution, or natural disaster.

regime A government, especially an authoritarian one.

Shiite A person who follows the Shiite sect of Islam, one of two main divisions in the religion.

Sunni A person who follows the Sunni sect of Islam, one of two main divisions in the religion.

FURTHER INFORMATION

Books

Fleming, Melissa. *A Hope More Powerful than the Sea: The Journey of Doaa Al Zamel*. New York: Flatiron Books, 2017.

Mustafa, Nujeen, with Christina Lamb. *Nujeen: One Girl's Incredible Journey from War-Torn Syria in a Wheelchair*. New York: Harper Wave, 2016.

Yazbek, Samar. *The Crossing: My Journey to the Shattered Heart of Syria*. London: Ebury Press, 2016.

Websites

Children of Syria

http://www.savethechildren.org/site/
c.8rKLIXMGIpl4E/b.7998857/k.D075/Syria.htm

Save the Children includes information about how the civil war has affected children, as well as their efforts to help.

CIA World Factbook: Syria

https://www.cia.gov/library/publications/
the-world-factbook/geos/print_sy.html

Find maps, information about Syria's history, and more on this website from the US Department of State.

I Am Syria

http://www.iamsyria.org

This nonprofit campaign seeks to educate the world about the war in Syria and includes suggestions for how to help.

Muslims Condemn

https://muslimscondemn.com

Inspired by the spreadsheet Heraa Hashmi made, Muslims Condemn compiles public records of Muslims condemning terrorist acts.

National Crime Prevention Council: Disaster Preparedness

http://www.ncpc.org/topics/preparedness

This site offers tips for young people, parents, and families so that you can prepare for emergencies.

Videos

"Demi Lovato and Muzoon Almellehan Chat Education, Refugees and Mental Health"

https://www.youtube.com/watch?v=rCjUd-ls4Ls

In addition to a successful music and acting career, Demi Lovato is a mental health advocate for refugees. Muzoon Almellehan has been called Syria's Malala Yousafzai; she is a teenage refugee who is working on improving education in emergencies. In this video, the two women discuss the issues they advocate for.

"The Girl Whose Shadow Reflects the Moon"

https://www.pri.org/stories/2016-03-10/syrian-
teens-auto-biographical-video-combines-
magical-imagery-and-gritty-reality

At age sixteen, a Syrian refugee who calls herself Walaa al-Alawi created a five-minute autobiographical film that has been screened at international film festivals.

"Inside ISIS' Self-Proclaimed Capital"

https://www.cbsnews.com/videos/inside-
isis-self-proclaimed-capital/

This video packs a lot of information from Raqqa, Syria, ISIS's self-proclaimed capital city, into its three and a half minutes.

BIBLIOGRAPHY

AFP. "Syria girls escape nightmare of war with Snow White fable." *Hindu*, May 27, 2017. http://www.thehindu.com/news/international/syria-girls-escape-nightmare-of-war-with-snow-white-fable/article18590493.ece.

Ashkar, Yasser. "Young Syrian inventor wins European Youth Award." OrientNet, January 28, 2017. http://orient-news.net/en/news_show/130726/0/Young-Syrian-inventor-wins-European-Youth-Award.

Attar, Lina Sergie. "Watching My Beloved Aleppo Rip Itself Apart." *New York Times*, August 13, 2016. https://www.nytimes.com/2016/08/14/opinion/sunday/watching-my-beloved-aleppo-rip-itself-apart.html.

——— . "Syrian Children Draw What Used to Be Home." *New York Times*, November 5, 2013. https://kristof.blogs.nytimes.com/2013/11/05/syrian-children-draw-what-used-to-be-home/.

Cafarella, Jennifer. "Why the most dangerous group in Syria isn't ISIS." CNN, February 26, 2016. http://www.cnn.com/2016/02/26/opinions/syria-isis-al-qaeda-nusra/index.html.

Callimachi, Rukmini. "ISIS and the Lonely Young American." *New York Times*, June 27, 2015. https://www.nytimes.

com/2015/06/28/world/americas/isis-online-recruiting-
american.html.

Campbell, Alexia Fernández. "Why ISIS Recruiting in America
Reached Historic Levels." *Atlantic*, December 6, 2015.
https://www.theatlantic.com/politics/archive/2015/12/
why-isis-recruiting-in-america-reached-historic-
levels/433560/.

Chappell, Bill. "2016 was worst year yet for children caught in
Syria's war, UNICEF says." MPR, March 13, 2017. https://
www.mprnews.org/story/2017/03/13/npr-syrias-civil-war-
killed-hundreds-of-children-in-2016-unicef-says.

Davison, John. "Syrian war creates child refugees and child
soldiers: report." Reuters, March 14, 2016. https://www.
reuters.com/article/us-mideast-crisis-syria-children-
idUSKCN0WG0R0.

Dutton, Judy. "Teen nuclear scientist fights terror," CNN,
last updated September 1, 2011. http://www.cnn.
com/2011/09/01/living/teen-nuclear-scientist/index.html.

Eaton, Joshua. "Teen Makes Spreadsheet of Muslim Groups
Denouncing Terrorism." *Teen Vogue*, November 14,
2016. https://www.teenvogue.com/story/teen-makes-
spreadsheet-muslim-groups-leaders-denouncing-
terrorism.

El Deeb, Sarah. "IS Militants Evacuate Last
    Stronghold in Syria to Government." AP News,
    November 9, 2017. https://www.apnews.com/
    f25ce410a4144fd8b8c9c96bc70ea18d.

Finnegan, Conor. "A look at the factions battling in Syria's
    civil war." ABC News, April 11, 2017. http://abcnews.
    go.com/International/inside-syrias-multiple-fighting-
    factions/story?id=46731830.

Hammer, Joshua. "Is a Lack of Water to Blame for the
    Conflict in Syria?" *Smithsonian*, June 2013. https://
    www.smithsonianmag.com/innovation/is-a-lack-of-
    water-to-blame-for-the-conflict-in-syria-72513729/.

Harkin, James. "Up to 186 Kurdish students kidnapped by
    Isis in northern Syria." *Guardian*, June 26, 2014. https://
    www.theguardian.com/world/2014/jun/26/186-kurdish-
    students-kidnapped-isis-syria.

——. "The Last Stand of the Heroic Kurds at Kobani."
    Newsweek, August 19, 2014. http://www.newsweek.
    com/2014/08/29/last-stand-kurdish-troopers-
    kobani-265522.html.

Hume, Tim. "Swedish teen rescued from ISIS speaks: 'It
    was really a hard life.'" CNN, February 24, 2016. http://
    www.cnn.com/2016/02/24/middleeast/swedish-teen-
    freed-from-isis/index.html.

Katt, Mais. "In Syrian war, all sides using child soldiers." UPI, June 27, 2016. https://www.upi.com/In-Syrian-war-all-sides-using-child-soldiers/4501466538098/.

Luck, Taylor. "ISIS puts a new twist on terror recruiting: big money." *Christian Science Monitor*, September 6, 2016. https://www.csmonitor.com/World/Middle-East/2016/0906/ISIS-puts-a-new-twist-on-terror-recruiting-big-money.

MacKinnon, Mark. "The Graffiti Kids Who Sparked the Syrian War." *Globe and Mail*, December 2, 2016. https://beta.theglobeandmail.com/news/world/the-graffiti-kids-who-sparked-the-syrian-war/article33123646/?ref=http://www.theglobeandmail.com&.

Mutter, Paul. "Kids on the Front Lines." *US News & World Report*, February 13, 2015. https://www.usnews.com/opinion/blogs/world-report/2015/02/13/the-rise-of-child-soldiers-in-syria.

Pinto, Tanya. "The 9 Groups Fighting in Syria." *Globalo*, April 13, 2016. http://www.globalo.com/the-9-groups-fighting-in-syria/.

Polk, William R. "Understanding Syria from Pre-Civil War to Post-Assad." *Atlantic*, December 10, 2013. https://www.theatlantic.com/international/archive/2013/12/understanding-syria-from-pre-civil-war-to-post-assad/281989/.

Schmidt, Michael S. "Canadian Killed in Syria Lives On as Pitchman for Jihadis." *New York Times*, July 15, 2014. https://www.nytimes.com/2014/07/16/world/middleeast/isis-uses-andre-poulin-a-canadian-convert-to-islam-in-recruitment-video.html.

Singh, Maanvi. "How Do Refugee Teens Build Resilience?" NPR, July 30, 2017. http://www.npr.org/sections/goatsandsoda/2017/07/30/540002667/how-do-refugee-teens-build-resilience.

Trianni, Francesca. "Watch: Syrian Children Talk Life as Child Soldiers." *Time*, June 22, 2014. http://time.com/2902332/syria-child-soldiers/.

Venkatesan. Supriya. "I'm 16 Years Old and I'm a Refugee." *Teen Vogue*, February 16, 2017. https://www.teenvogue.com/story/im-16-years-old-and-im-a-syrian-refugee.

Williams, Holly. "U.S.-backed Syrian forces say victory in ISIS capital Raqqa is days away." CBS News, October 8, 2017. https://www.cbsnews.com/news/us-backed-syrian-forces-say-victory-in-isis-capital-raqqa-is-days-away/.

INDEX

ABOUT THE AUTHOR

Kristin Thiel lives in Portland, Oregon, where she is a writer and editor of books, articles, and documents for publishers, individuals, and businesses. She has worked on many of the books in the So, You Want to Be A ... series, which offers career guidance for kids and is published by Beyond Words, an imprint of Simon & Schuster. She was the lead writer on a report for her city about funding for high school dropout prevention. Thiel has judged YA book contests and managed before-school and afterschool literacy programs for AmeriCorps VISTA.